Doctor Chronos

by

Othello

Gooden Jr.

Special

thanks

to:

Evie Wright

"For man does not know his time. Just as fish are caught in an evil net and birds are caught in a trap, so the sons of men are ensnared in a time of disaster, when it suddenly overtakes them."

~ (Ecclesiastes 9:12)

Chapter 1

04 - 2021

It's been one wild ride, and I can totally not believe how far I've come. I figure it's probably time to chronicle all of the events that brought me this far. You know, before I begin to forget. I can't believe I've come thiis far. I can see myself that year, shortly after obtaining my doctorate... I guess I have to start at the beginning.

I just feel the memories come rushing in. It's been such a crazy time, getting to this point. I decided to write because they are so overwhelming, I need to share it somehow. I remember the first time I had this idea. It wasn't originally mine, of course. I was having dinner with a few friends while I was doing my PhD program, and one of them brought it up. I can't remember the specifics because it was a few years ago.

But I remember thinking about it and going something like, "Hmmm, ain't that an idea." I totally forgot about it then, until maybe months later in a class, when one of our professors mentioned it again. It was then that the idea grabbed hold of me, and I started doing my research on the topic. I mean, this was something that had never been done before, despite the various attempts that had gone into it by so many people.

The world of science, especially physics and Quantum Mechanics in particular, was a pretty scary one sometimes. I had to tell people about this to get some help, especially financially, but i couldn't do that without coming up with something worthwhile.

So I started working. It's funny, thinking about those times. There were nights I barely slept an hour. I holed up in my lab, working till I dropped off at my desk, and then waking up just to continue the grind. I took my bath when I couldn't bear to live with my own stink, and lived on pizza and soda.

I didn't even realize how much time passed until one morning when there was a knock on my door. I still remember Zyra coming in and hitting me with her fist, again and again and again for a while. She said something like "Do you know how worried I've been?" And told me that if I was going to hibernate in my office, the least I could have done was call her or send her a message.

I told her I was sorry for worrying her, and then we went out for dinner... after she took my clothes to the Laundromat and guilt tripped me into cleaning up my lab. Zyra was the first person I ever told about the work I was doing. She was so supportive.

My little sister... She was the best friend any girl could have. It always made me sad that we met so late in life. But that was another accusation I could level against my dad... But that's a story for later. We talked at length about what my research would mean if I was actually successful at it, and then she made me promise to get at least one good meal a week and call her if I needed anything—that little mother hen!

It took more months of work before I finally came up with something I felt was presentable enough. Something I could finally bring my colleagues in on. I started out with a couple of friends. Like I expected, they were all skeptical at the beginning. But the more I'd done on it to show them, the more surprised and accepting they became. They encouraged me to go speak with some other people about it, and I somehow garnered enough support for the work.

Then I had to go before the board and present my research in order to gain some funding. It had been pretty hard, staring in their faces, I remember. I was so nervous, I kept stumbling through the first part of my presentation.

Then I heard a buzz from my phone which was lying on the podium before me. The screen flashed on, and it was a message from Zyra. "It's gonna go great, sis. You'll do fine, and they'll all be so wowed, they'll empty their pockets."

I can't ever forget it. It was like I just this buzz of energy from who knew where, and I got my confidence back, became calm, and just did as Zyra said. I wowed them. Getting the grant to continue my research did not surprise me. It wasn't enough for me to go the whole nine yards, but it would help me get far enough that I could approach the bigger organizations.

The day I got it, I called Zyra to tell her. She was so happy, she laughed for like an hour. Okay, I'm exaggerating. Maybe five minutes. I decided in the exhilaration of the moment to ask her and dad out to dinner. The three of us were rarely together anymore, and it was dad's fault. Totally.

Still, I had some hope that maybe when he heard that I actually got some money for the 'horse manure', as he called the work I was doing, he would be proud. Or at least, swallow his previous words. Well, despite all I wished for that night, I'm sure you probably know that, like every other time dad and I end up in the same room, it didn't go well.

I promised myself that I wouldn't get angry at dinner that night. I did the whole meditation, yoga thing so that I would be in a good frame of mind. Plus, I just got my first grant for the project. Nothing could bring my mood down.

Then again, I guess I was just overestimating my self control. Dad was so frustrating. And that's a pretty mild word to use for him, honestly. You'd think that after all the years, all the work I've put into the field, he would trust me when I told him that I had done some pretty big calculations over the past few months and come up with a breakthrough.

I can't forget what he said and did when I first told him about what I was working on. It was over a year ago, but still fresh in my mind. We went to dinner in one of the best restaurants where we lived. The Lunar Space Station in orbit of the moon was a pretty cool place to live.

There weren't many people living here, compared to other places mankind has colonized, like Lunar Prime and some privately owned outer-space living habitats, so there was pretty much enough space for everything you wanted to do. After all, the LSS, what it's commonly referred to as, is the largest and first of its kind. We even have artificial gravity generators, invented by a Korean MIT Cybernetics Intern named Michelle Pyun. She transferred to Lunarian University a few years along with a few of her colleagues, Conner Evans and Asa Ravenscraft. All were in the same major and both contributed to the creation of her "baby". Her patented Pyun AG System is now embedded in core systems of Lunar Prime and the LSS. Lastly, compared to my lab space alone, I know heads of government whose offices weren't half as big. Perks.

The first part of the evening went really well. We talked about the different things we were all doing. Dad told us he was in the process of expanding of Norman Labs, the family owned clinical laboratory business, with an acquisition, and then we celebrated Zyra's promotion at this Law Firm in Sector A of the LSS called Raylor and Associates. It was owned by our cousin, Raylor Mellis. She was now COO of it after the previous one retired. I didn't want to talk about my news, not during the early part of the dinner. And thank heavens I waited, really.

Okay, my arms are getting tired already. Guess I'll continue the rest of the story later.

Chapter 2

05 - 2021

Yeah so... In my last entry, I left off where I invited dad and Zyra out for dinner. So after waiting and waiting, and ignoring the questioning glances Zyra threw at me, I finally just cut dad short in the middle of his rant about how the people he was buying out were already going under and he was trying to save them.

"So dad, I finally made a headway in my research!" Zyra started clapping, but then stopped abruptly at the look in dad's eyes. He wasn't angry or sad or anything like that. Maybe if that was it, my stomach wouldn't have been so jittery.

No, there was scorn in his eyes. "You made a headway? Just like you did that time two years ago when you got a loan to test one of your mad bunny schemes and I had to pay back?"

I winced. Despite how I told myself to stay strong, I still flinched at his words. I forced my face to stay neutral, to just look at him without speaking. As always, Zyra came to bat for me.

"Dad, come on. Sigma worked her back to the bone on odd jobs to pay you back. It's not like she still owes you or anything. You don't have to bring it up." My heart wanted to burst in gratitude, but I couldn't even tell her thank you. I had to keep my mouth shut now, keep my words to myself and lock down my emotions. If I didn't, I knew I'd have burst into tears.

"Well, she wouldn't have had to pay me back if she wasn't running off getting her fingers into that stuff she calls a job, now, would she?"

"It is a job, dad. And a highly respected one for that matter. For once, you should be happy for Sigma. I mean, she got a grant, for God's sake. On this same job that you are always demeaning."

"Oh?" Dad said, finally losing his sneer. He raised his brows instead. "Well, how much did you get?"

"This is just the start. I mean, it's not like I have advanced really well in the project yes, so they just gave me a little, to see what I would come up with." His brows were still raised, so I finally told him.

It was silent around the table for a long, long minute. Then dad burst into laughter so loud, people all around the restaurant turned to look at us. I turned slightly to get a read on Zyra's expression. She was sitting there, mouth open, staring at my dad like he was a second moon that grew out of the moon through binary fission or something.

I would have laughed, but my stomach was clenched tight. I stayed still instead, waiting to hear what he would say. No, I wasn't anxious, or sad, or nervous, or something. I wasn't. At all.

"Finally, dad lost his breath, and the laughter ended just as fast as it started. "You know, I don't know if I've ever mentioned a friend's son to you. Can't exactly recall his name right now. You see, that boy has spent barely three years in the field since he got done with his microbiology degree. Last I heard, he got a grant for working on some antiviral drug to a virus people living on the LSS are particularly susceptible to. And it was worth maybe six times what you just mentioned."

"Daddy-"

"Enough, Zyra. I've told your sister often enough that she is wasting her time in that field. I mean, it's not like you're doing anything that benefits society. You're working on time-travel? Who cares about stuff like that?"

"Dad, you tell me there aren't some things in your past you wouldn't want to change if you had the opportunity to," Zyra threw back. "Or you aren't interested in maybe seeing the future."

I couldn't speak. I think maybe I had gone mute for those minutes. I was just sitting there, staring at dad as he continued speaking. I should have been used to this by now, I told myself. Ever since high school, and especially after I got into college and majored in Quantum Physics. Even now, after graduating. I started working with some of the best minds in my field, he still keeps harping on about how what I do is of no benefit to anyone whatsoever.

"Even if I did have things I want to change, it's past. Who wants to waste their lives on trying to get to a past that has already been lived?"

"Dad-"

"Look, Zyra, just forget it, okay?" I finally burst out. Dad continued to rant about how I'm wasting my life on things that aren't important. As always, his main point is how all we do in my field is provide fodder for writers to build imaginary worlds and how we contribute nothing, only eat up money with fruitless research.

After a while, I can't hold my tears back anymore. But I didn't want to give him the satisfaction of knowing that his words hurt me, so I grabbed my jacket and told them I was leaving.

Just as I walked out, I could hear Zyra telling him, "You know, for once in your life you could actually act like you are proud of your daughter."

Every time she defends me against my dad, it always reminds me of when we first met. I had just turned eighteen, and was preparing to meet with my academic advisor at Lunarian University about furthering my education for my graduate degree. It was early afternoon when I heard a knock on our front door. I was the only one home, so I went to see who it was.

When I opened the door and looked out, I saw this young lady who looked so much like me, it was unbelievable. I just wordlessly opened the door and let her in. It was awkward at first, talking to her. Within a few minutes, we were chatting like friends. By the time dad came home that evening, I knew all about his infidelity to mom. I confronted him about it, but as he always was with everything, he tried to absolve himself of the blame. It was that day that 18 year old Zyra came to live with us, and it remains one of the best days of my life.

That night, when I heard her tell dad to act like he was proud of me for once, I wanted to tell her she was fighting a losing battle. I cried all the way home. I didn't need him to be proud of me or anything. I was fine doing my own thing. I didn't need him for anything—And I tried so hard to ignore the little voice within me that was calling me a liar.

Chapter 3

06 - 2021

Today is one of those cold spring days. You think winter and the cold are finally gone, and then you wake up one morning almost frozen to death. The cold days are getting more few and far between though, but it makes it all the more colder when it sneaks up on you. I don't like it when it's this cold. Then you have the LSS's environmental controls emulating North American Mid-Western winters! So annoying! I'd prefer tropical temperatures. Don't tell Zyra. She loves winter. She's weird like that. The only thing I fight with her on besides working too much is how she keeps the individual thermostat temp in the freezing range.

Anyway, at dinner that night, the sound of my father's laughter was probably what pushed me over. I became so possessed with trying to prove him wrong. I knew that to get a bigger grant and complete my research would take loads of work. And work I did. I don't remember ever working as hard as I did all those months. I just kept digging, just kept working. But if there was a lesson I learned during that time, it was that hard work was only about half of the battle. There were so many other factors.

First, it only took a few months before the money I got from that first grant ran out. And since all I had to show for all my spending was a lot of failed calculations and experiments, it was difficult. I started looking for investors, business people who wanted to get access to patents and stuff like that. The first one I sent my proposal to didn't even bother calling me. Another sent me communication saying politely that they weren't interested. To be honest, I'd have preferred not to get it at all, because I'd felt so excited when I saw the company's logo and all. Then to have all my hopes dashed...

Some others gave me audience, but then dismissed my ideas as nothing but theoretical nonsense, and said they had no merit. There was no point investing in something doomed to failure. After getting this reply from more than six interviews, I got so frustrated. I just sat in the park crying one early morning. It was shortly after that I got a call from a small company I had never approached. They told me they'd heard about my research, and they were interested.

I was so happy, I met the board and company execs and techs, and for days, I went over all of my research and work with them. In my desperation, I even left copies of the work I had done with them, except for a few things I wanted to hold back. One of the sacred rules most researchers in my field, and probably others, had, was to never allow anyone full access to all your work. Not even your spouse. A lot of backstabbing went on, and you didn't want freely hand the knife over to anyone.

Barely a month later, while I was still waiting for the company's decision as to whether they would give me the grant or not, I went for a small get-together with colleagues. I was talking to a few of them about my work when someone joined our group and overhead.

Then he cut in. I think he said something like "You're working on time-travel? Maybe you'll like to communicate with Dalton Fox. I think the company just started doing some research into it. I have a friend who's a physicist there, and he says they are making a headway, due to some new research they did."

It froze my insides like someone suddenly shoved a barrel of snow down my throat. All through dinner, I told myself not to jump to conclusions, that maybe this guy didn't get the right information, or the physicist had somehow missed out on some critical information, like my name.

However, when I tried contacting the company for some communication and got blocked at every angle, I realized that it was really happening. My research had been stolen.

I never imagined something like this could happen. I got a lawyer. My first choice for one was Zyra but she was busy on another case at this time. We worked through the case over and again until we were sure we had something foolproof. Then we went to court. Before we could even start the thing properly, the company brought in their own experts and stuff, and the court ruled that since they already applied to the government for the rights to the research and I could prove that I had started all of it before them, I had no rights.

During that period, there were nights I cried myself to sleep. Zyra was still in Lunar Prime for the next few months and I didn't want to bother her with the details. But somehow my dad found out and he sent me an email.

I deleted it almost immediately after reading it, but I still remember some of the words. "Stupid" and "foolhardy" were some of the softest ones. I thought my world had ended, until one morning someone woke me up and told me to check the business news. I didn't feel like. I hadn't felt like doing anything those weeks. Still, I knew it had to be pretty important.

There was a reporter in the news, and then I could see the name of the company that had stolen my dream written at the top of the screen. At first I felt like kicking the TV screen to the ground, bashing it with a hammer or a bat or whatever else I could find until...

Hey, that's my alarm. I have to go get ready for the company event. Oh, joy. Guess I'll continue with this later.

Chapter 4

07 - 2021

I've slept through the day. I never drink, but maybe that's because I've trained myself to say no whenever Zyra invites me to a party. And for good reason too. Just look at yesterday. She guilt tripped me into attending the after-party, and now I'm going to have to spend a week treating hangover headaches. If I didn't love that girl so much, I don't know what I'd do to her. Yeah, so back to the whole journey thing. Well, I finally got over my murderous thoughts and paid attention to what the newscaster was saying.

For the millionth time in only a few weeks, tears began to run down my face. But this time, I wasn't crying in pain, you know. It was actual joy. So apparently, the entire systems of Fox Den Interplanetary were down. They had been working on the time-travel project that had become so popular when it blew up in their faces. Literally. System failure. The entire unit exploded and caught on fire. Almost burned down the whole building. Boy, was karma a crazy dog.

Hearing what happened to them and how they were likely going to abandon the project got me going again. It was difficult on two levels, I remember. First, I still had to look for investors, despite the fiasco that happened the last time I did. Getting over the fear and wariness that had aroused in me was a big job. Zyra and a few other friends had given me quite a lot of pep talks back then.

The second hurdle I had to cross was external this time. The failure of the Dalton Fox Project at Fox Den Interplanetary became such big news, when I told the potential investors I met with what I was working on, they just laughed in my face.

It took more weeks, trying to still get some work done despite the limits I had with funding. Finally, I got so desperate, I began to do something I never thought I'd resort to. My short stories, many of the ones I'd been writing at that time, well, I began to submit them to magazines.

I'd write stories with me as the central character in different scenarios and then email them to editors of magazines, earn some money. It was still much too little though, and there was only so much I could do without money, and then I just to keep searching for someone to invest in the project.

Finally, I got in contact with someone who told me they would get back to me. Honestly, I wasn't really expecting much, but only a few days later I received communication for a net meeting. Apparently, this person who was interested in my work did not live on the LSS like I did. When I tried to contact them with the details that I got, all I got were "mail daemon" error messages. I tried and tried to call and text, but I got no response.

Until the next week, that was. The week I got a text message that called me a fraud for stealing the idea of whoever sent it. The next few days were pretty horrible. I lost about half of the money in my bank account. Not that I had so much there, but now it was barely enough to live on. They kept taking out a little by little around the same time every week and funneling it to another account.

When I went to complain at my bank they told me my account had been hacked. It was pretty horrible, realizing that my account wasn't safe anymore. I finally got a new one at another bank. The next message I received arrived in my email. I took the case to the Lunar law enforcement. The person who sent them said I was a fraud who had a pipe dream, and that I should give up.

I felt so unsafe in my lab after I received threatening letters in my mailbox. I told dad I was moving back into the house. Not that I had ever officially left, actually. I just got tired of hearing him saying that I've put my life on hold to chase after something that would never happen.

I can't recall how many times dad harped on about me being out of college and unmarried, living in his house. And okay, maybe some of my guy friends asked me out, but I was really too busy to date anyone. It was better to just hold them off and remain friends than to accept someone's invitation only for them to later discover they weren't the one for me.

My headache's coming back big time right now. Guess I'll continue writing later, once I've slept a bit.

Chapter 5

08 - 2021

Another dawn. At least my headache is almost totally gone now. I wish I had Zyra's constitution. The girl could party three days straight without skipping a beat. I just loved my lab and my work.

When dad asked what happened after I moved back in, I told him all about the messages and stuff. He thought about the case for quite a while, before telling me it was probably someone associated with Dalton Fox that hired a hacker. He said it was likely that they gave them my bank info. Quantum Encryption hackers only needed the account number and routing to hack into any bank through their SSN. I also read on the net how the identity of those who did that stuff were rarely ever found out because of how sophisticated their security and firewall protocols were to hide their exact location.

Then, when I thought I'd garnered enough sympathy from dad, he finally started talking again about how even if time-travel was somehow even possible, I'd probably not even be the one to come up with a way to do it. All I was doing was wasting time and digging myself more into more and more student debt.

I remember that I got so mad at dad's words, I began to search for an investor even more because I had something to prove. And as soon as I found anyone ready to help me out, I took their help. I kept working and working and working. Somewhere in my mind, I told myself that I could do this. Flying had once been an impossibility for the people who lived on Earth. Now it was an everyday thing.

I was going to work on this until I got what I wanted. I had this buzz that I was getting close, and then I sidetracked my own work by doing some very closely related project. I figured that there would probably be some side effects of time traveling, and so I wanted to try to create something that would ameliorate those. I knew if I didn't do it now, before I finally worked everything out, I would be too impatient, and heaven only knew what would happen.

I worked for weeks and weeks until I finally was done creating it. I called it the Quantum Chain. It was a necklace that's supposed to protect me from the effects of the timeline changes, whatever time period I found myself in. I did all the work I could do, but I had no chance of discovering if it really worked, and worked well, until I actually used it. So I placed it in a container and hid it as well as I could.

Then I returned my focus to syncing the Quantum Chain with the small wristwatch I used to initiate the time-travel protocol with. It took more weeks, and more weeks, before I worked out the code. The day I wrote down the last letter of the equation, I sat back in my chair with disbelief.

After years of working on the same project, after tons of failures, after all the harsh and demeaning comments I'd had on my work, I couldn't believe I had finally done it. I went to where I had kept my Quantum Chain, and took it out almost reverently. Then I put it on, sat in front of my computer, and began the time-travel process. I wasn't sure whether I had done it, whether it worked, not at first. Truthfully, I didn't expect it to. Everywhere, everything was the same. My apartment was still littered with papers and files, like I had been working on for a long time. I probably needed a break now. I just never really took one. Ever. Probably never will either.

I felt a vague sense of disorientation, and I didn't understand why. It was probably because I'd been working for hours already with no food, or at least that was what I thought. Suddenly, deciding to actually go out and see the sun, I grabbed my cellphone and house keys and walked out the room. Yet the disorientation continued to where my vision became very blurry. I searched my room for something until I came across the thing I was looking for-a pair of glasses.

“Glasses? When did I ever need these?” I sighed. That was a very drastic change. After I put them on, I looked through the pictures on my phone. I was curious about something. Have I always wore glasses? My phone showed every selfie I took of myself in various colored frame glasses. My favorite color was fuchsia. I got a couple of plants by the same name around my home also! My phone was loaded with pictures with me taking pictures of myself and my plants.

So I wear glasses now? Check. But I admit, now I look even nerdier, not just with the degree to back my 'nerdiness' up... Ha!

Then I got a whiff of my own scent. It was enough to make me grimace in disgust. I took my bath, brushed my teeth, and changed clothes. That's when I noticed a medium-sized tattoo in the center of my chest after I saw myself in my bathroom's mirror. It was the Greek letter Sigma in a red color. The tat was layered in different shades of it to look embossed. The center-most layer was the lightest.

Okay, when did I get this?! Several months ago was what came to my mind. Never thought I would get one of these. Things you learn in a new timeline about yourself... Huh! After pondering over the small things about myself that was different, including my obsession with all things pink, I tossed my laundry into two big bin bags. Yeah, okay, I'd become a slob. How you like that? You would too if you were trying to figure out the perfect calculations and whatnot needed for time-travel.

I took the clothes to the Laundromat, then walked on for a bit to get to my favorite restaurant in the neighborhood. I stepped in there and approached the counter. When I looked around the place, I wondered how it was possible that the placed had changed in barely any time. Though I hadn't really come in recently because of how busy I was.

Still, how come I couldn't even recognize any of the workers there? I was already ordering my food, when the news came on. I think my mouth totally dropped open. It was 2020. No. No way. That wasn't possible. I didn't do it... did I? Had my dream finally become a reality? I called the attention of the guy at the counter. "I'm so sorry, what is today's date?" I asked him.

"Today's the nineteenth," he replied.

I wanted to ask him for the full date, but I knew it would be really odd, and if my suspicions were true, this was so not the time to draw attention to myself. I changed my order to takeaway, and I headed home. I dumped my food on the table in the living room and probably never ate it. I then walked to my room and began to search through all of it. Some of my research was still there, but almost nothing I'd done in the past few years.

I was trying to figure it all out, just standing there in the center of the room, when my phone rang. It was Zyra. After letting out a deep breath, I picked up the phone. "Hi Zyra," I said. I didn't know if I could tell her yet. I decided to just wait.

"Hey, cuzzo," she said. That made my senses reel. I'm Zyra's cousin here? I try to keep my voice and breathing as natural as possible. "I just called to check up on you. I was sure you'd have been so buried in research, and you've probably not eaten all day. Go get something to fill up your stomach, Sigma."

"I actually just got in from buying dinner," I told her. She gave a loud yell.

"I'm so proud of you, cuz. Hey, did I tell you Will was back in town?" Zyra asked.

"Will? Which Will?" I asked, and then clasped my palm to my face. I wasn't supposed to act like I didn't know stuff.

"Uh, hello? My brother. Seems like I need to come dig you out of those books once in a while."

Thank God she attributed my mistake to that, I didn't know what I would have done. I pushed away the thought of Zyra being my cousin and having a brother. I'd have to think about them later. Taking advantage of the opportunity though, I finally asked what I'd been dying to know.

Chapter 6

09 - 2021

I wrote for so long in my last entry. It's been a while since I did that. Guess now that I'm not doing it so much anymore, it's a bit tiring. So, I asked Zyra what was the date? The full date. It was late March, 2020. I totally couldn't believe it. I had finally done it. I'd done it, and I had come out on the other side. I thought back to the months and years of slaving over this dream. And I took a deep breath, lifting my face to the ceiling.

"Cuzzo? You even listening to me?"

"Yes, Zyra, yes I am. I was just lost in thought for a moment." I paid more attention as she talked about us having dinner together the next night. I knew it would be an opportunity to learn more about this family, the things that had changed since... Well, since I traveled through time into this past.

The next evening, I'd only been in the house for a minute when I realized that things were so much different than I had ever imagined. First of all, the house itself was like something out of a fairy tale. It was evening, and so the lights gave a soft glow that filled the house with warm energy. Plus the sheer size of the property... Even for a plot of land this size on a Space Station was truly magnificent!

The next thing that gave me a haunch that things were totally different in this era was when a servant dressed in a pretty cool uniform came to open the door. Everything screamed old money, deep pockets. I wanted to ask for Zyra, to let her guide me in this suddenly strange situation. I wasn't a coward though. I glanced around, but the servant had withdrawn. He probably expected me to know where to go.

I walked into the living room, and the first picture I saw stunned me. It was a picture of two people, Zyra and the man I knew as General William Raylor Mellis Sr. Not that there was anything extraordinary about the name. It was the fact that he was a billionaire veteran that shook me to the core.

By the time I'd looked at every picture is there, I realized that I was in way over my head. I had entered an alternate reality. That was the only explanation I could think of for how my sister... erm... my cousin's father was a billionaire, and a General at that!

It also seemed from the pictures that Zyra was older than I. I wasn't sure by how much, but I'd learn more as time went on. My phone rang just then. It was Zyra. "Are you here yet?"

"Yes, I am."

"Then what are you waiting for? Come on up," she yelled, almost splitting my eardrum.

I didn't know where she was, but I assumed she meant the upper floor of the house and climbed up the stairs. I'd knocked on four doors before one finally opened up to Zyra. When I saw her, it took me a lot to keep my shock under control. She couldn't have been less than five years older than I was.

I was so shocked, when she threw arms around me, it took me a long moment to respond. I walked round the room as she talked, looking at the knickknacks scattered around. A picture of her high school graduating class hung on her wall.

I noted the year, then did my calculations, and realized that she was ten years older than I was. The age difference probably would have affected our reactions to each other, if Zyra hadn't been really witty and humorous.

She soon had me laughing at something that had happened at work some weeks before. As I watched her dress, I suddenly felt under-dressed. I hadn't prepared to come to the house of a billionaire or something.

When I said that to Zyra, she just laughed and told me not to worry about it. I heard a bell ring from somewhere in the house and assumed it was the front door. At least until Zyra said, "C'mon, that's our summons to dinner."

They rang bells for meals. I shook my head as I followed my cousin down the hall. And as we entered the room, I saw General William Raylor Mellis Sr. in the flesh. He's the founder of the Lunarian Society and the Lunar Space Station. He was beside a woman who I knew from the pictures was his wife.

I tried to act really normally, smiling and shaking his hand as if I'd seen him a million times before.

From the door another person burst into the room. "Hey, guys." Will Junior was probably the most handsome young man I'd ever seen. If he wasn't Zyra's older brother—which meant familial connection, I'd date him. Everyone called him RJ.

Dinner was fun, with Zyra and RJ throwing teasing comments at each other, then at me and their parents. I spent most of my time just listening and trying to work out all of the dynamics of their relationship. The General, as what everyone called RJ's father, even in the future where I was from was an absolute playboy. He had several marriages, and divorces, but no children. The picture I got of him now, as I watched the family, was one of love and affection. It was odd.

I also imagined what my family would be like. I knew Norman would still be my dad, and that was because I saw pictures of dad and the General. I needed to do some checking into my past as soon as possible, to learn what I had to know. I also didn't think I had any siblings. If I did, their pictures should have been here there. Unfortunately, I didn't. Though it hurt at first, at least I didn't lose Zyra. Even in this timeline, she's still my favored relative out of all of them—the one I felt understood me the most.

Chapter 7

10 - 2021

I keep stopping abruptly, don't I? Well, this time I had to mail something over to a colleague, and then I didn't just keep writing.

So that night at dinner, Zyra noticed how quiet I was and asked me why when we walked back to her room. "Oh, nothing. Just a little bit tired. Probably work."

"You work too hard, sweetheart. I've told you before, I know what you're doing is important, but you need to have time to rest. I wish you would have come with me on that vacation."

"It was a work retreat, Zyra. I would have been on my own and it would have been pretty boring. Besides, I had some-"

"Research. You'll always have research to do, Sigma. But you won't be young forever. There is the time to work, but now's the time to play, okay?"

I nodded obediently, even though the knowing glance she shot me told me that we both knew I wasn't going to change my lifestyle for anything. We talked some more, and then she told her driver to take me home.

When I got home, I went snooping. I checked out pictures and files and whatever I could find in the house that. When I realized that dad still owned Norman Labs, an idea suddenly began to develop in my mind. I didn't need my father's approval anymore. I definitely did not need it now.

But if I could get it on a thesis about my success in time-travel, I'll be able to take it back to the future with me and show him, along with some video and audio recordings. Then I'd make him eat his words about how time-travel was a useless thing to waste I time on.

It was surprisingly easy to orchestrate everything. The Mellis name carried a lot of weight in this area, but I decided to go with a fake name instead. I used an image inducer that would change my looks, and then applied for the job at Lunarian University. I also changed to contact lenses.

I worked there for a short while, using the period to fine tune the thesis I wanted to submit to Norman Labs at a Science and Technology Conference. After a couple of months, I finally sent it in. Dad sent a personal email directly to me telling me—or well, Amy Meadows—that he wanted to see me for an interview.

It was the first time I was meeting my father in this time period, and at first I felt nervous. But during the interview, I got my confidence back. It was when he offered me the job that I stood up and turned off my image inducer.

Dad looked pretty shocked, but he wasn't angry like I expected. Instead, once the expression of surprise cleared off his face, he broke into a smile instead.

"Why am I not surprised?" He said.

"You were surprised," I threw back at him.

"Well, I did have a hunch that it could be you masquerading or something. You or your alter ego acted pretty much the same way."

"You always said that what I did didn't really matter, that it was all theoretical mumbo jumbo. But you are willing to hire someone else to do this. You even rejected my application when I applied to the family business using my own name!" My tone probably sounded really accusatory, bit I didn't care. "Why couldn't I be enough for you? I'm your daughter. You treat everyone else better, like my work doesn't matter. Like I don't matter."

"Yes, I know I did, Sigma. And I'm so, so sorry. I never meant to make you feel like you didn't matter. The truth is, you matter so much to me, more than anyone else. I pushed you so hard because I wanted you to succeed, but I never meant to take it that far. I'm sorry."

I didn't want to accept his apology, because he had been a real jerk to me all my life. My mother even left him because of irreconcilable differences—he's so dang stubborn! Still, I figured that two wrongs didn't make a right. I didn't want to be like my father. "I forgive you, dad," I said, and then walked out.

I figured I had done what I needed to do here. Dad had acknowledged my work in this past. It was time to go back to the future. I went back to my lab and set in the equations to take me back to the future.

Everything looks different when I got back. Changed. Panicking, I check through my house, my room, everything is different. I start reading through the documents I found on my electronic diary, checking through the files I had in the room.

I think I changed the future. I find documents talking about how General Mellis funded my time-travel research, and there was no mention of me getting other investors or things like that.

I also find no evidence of the fictional stories I used to write, not in any magazines or any such thing. When I go home after a long day at the lab, dad is there with my mom. When I tell them about the time-travel thing and show both the evidence, they tell me that they're proud of me, proud that I have been able to live my dream.

It's a pretty wonderful, how things are going now, don't you think?

CHAPTER 8

11 - 2021

Almost immediately after I arrived back in the new present, I began to hear stories that scare me. The first time I heard her name, I almost laughed. Zyra had come to visit, and she looked so much different, more beautiful but more reserved, and there were stress lines all over her face.

I hugged her for a long time, and when I pulled away she gave me a funny look. She was probably wondering why I did that. I hadn't yet found the time to tell her about my time-traveling adventure and everything that had happened, but I figured I needed to soon. I knew I had changed things in the future, but I had no idea how much until we sat down to dinner with dad and they began talking.

"So, how was your day, Zyra?" Dad asked, a concerned look on his face. I turned to look at Zyra, wondering if she had a hard case she was working on. Often, Zyra did Pro Bono cases, and then she would come home sad, because of how much the underprivileged were treated.

Thinking that was the case, I was about to put my arm around her for a hug, when she shook her head. "Keeping him safe has been such a big deal. Just yesterday, we discovered that one of his new aides, someone we had vetted and I personally interviewed, has turned out to be a traitor."

I glance between the both of them, trying to follow the conversation, but it was confusing. What on Lunar could Nina have to do with keeping anyone safe?

"It is not your fault, Zyra," Dad replied. "I know things look pretty hard right now, but it will get better."

"Of course it's my fault!" she burst out. Zyra was usually the more emotional of the both of us, but seeing her flare up that way shocked me more than anything. Seeing her breakdown in tears as the words started gushing out made me hurt.

"Of course, it's my fault. He appointed me as Chief of Staff, and I allowed someone to infiltrate his private life so closely that he could have been killed at any point. I feel like I'm not good at my job. How am I supposed to keep him safe if I can't even take care of something as little as an appointment?

The threats from Naira are growing daily. I'm so afraid of what that woman could do, what she's planning. The aide had been sending her secret information about where the General would be at any point in time." She paused, wiping her eyes with the back of her hands.

That made me realize that I had been staring at the both of them, dumbfounded. Muttering an excuse, I walked to the bathroom to get wipes. Zyra was Chief of Staff of the General? That was shocking enough. There was something else going on, something that was scaring my cousin, and I needed to find out what it was. Taking the box of wipes out, I walked back to the dining room and handed them over to Zyra. She gave me a thankful glance and nod, then cleaned up her face.

"Okay," I said, realizing that they had both stopped talking. "I need you both to please clear up some things for me. You mentioned something about Naira, and the name does sound very familiar, but then you said something about her infiltrating the General's office, and so I want some clarity on all of that."

Zyra shot me a strange look. "But Sigma, we talked about a lot of this on the phone like a week ago. Plus, you always follow the news, especially since Naira began her campaigns and stuff."

Dad and I exchanged glances, and then her expression changed. "Wait, there is something going on here that I don't know about, isn't it?" Zyra asked.

I nodded. "I'd rather not go into it right now. I will tell you," I added when she looked hurt. "I promise I'll tell you, Zyra. Later on, in private." There were things about my research that I felt only comfortable enough to share with her. Despite the fact that I had forgiven my father for everything he did and said, and I knew he wasn't the same man, not in this present, it was still hard for me to let him know a lot about me. I had this secret fear that he would go back to being the way he used to be.

"Alright." She looked happier already. "So what do you want to know?"

"Who is this Naira person? I mean, I do know if one Naira, I think her name is Naira Hill-Adega or something like that." At Zyra's nod, I knew my face went blank with shock. "Wait, I don't think I'm getting you very well. You mean she's the person you have been talking about all along?"

"Why are you acting like you don't get all of this stuff?" Zyra asked. She looked perplexed, and I didn't want to go into all of the details yet. Finally, I asked if we could meet for lunch the next day.

Dad was silent, only watching us. I agreed, and then we dropped the topic, talking about other things that had been happening. Zyra told me she'd met a good guy, but the amount of work she had on her plate due to the security problems didn't let her have time to go out with anyone.

I consoled her, silently making up my mind that I had to go and do some deep research into exactly what was going on right now. The way Zyra and Dad spoke, it seemed like things were really terrible, and that scared me.

Perhaps, my going back into the past hadn't been the best recourse after all.

CHAPTER 9

12 - 2021

Things have been getting really crazy around here. I could not believe how different it all was. That evening, after Zyra left, I went to the old shelf where dad usually kept his newspapers and took out a number of the most recent ones to do some research.

I could still remember Naira Hill-Adega—widow of a politician named Vern Malik Hill. She had a strong South African accent. Yet Vern was from North America and his accent was proof there of. Sources say they met each other on one of her interplanetary "preaching" tours several years ago. I had seen her in the news once or twice before I traveled back in time but the Naira I new was single but was some sort of Televangelist. The first time I heard about something of the latter, I shook my head and smirked. Naira was a Seven Day of Venice preacher, and often referred to herself as Apostle Naira. It was also the term her adherents called her.

I never really believed all of that stuff anyway, despite how many people she had converted into following her. When I was a child, I had learned the stories of all the apostles. Paul, Peter and the rest of them. The last apostle was John, and he died after being exiled on an island for his faith. Besides, the

Apostles back then did a lot of things. They healed people and all of that good stuff. Naira obviously wasn't doing much of it. If anything, the stories about how she'd healed had turned out to be false. So when I saw all of her vanity and how she tried to make people believe she was special or something, I just feel it was all stupid.

However, the news that solidified my notion of her was when I saw her in the news the second time. There had been an exposé on her, showing her coming out of different hotels in different places with different men. There had also been stories that some of those men were married and other stuff like that.

Immediately I read all of it, I totally wrote her off in my mind as a fake. She was obviously a very adulterous person, and the Apostles I learned about completely condemned the practice—Ya now, 'Thou Shall Not Commit Adultery?' So there was no way I was going to believe Naira was a real Apostle.

When I started reading the papers, I didn't expect to see anything good. But I was more shocked than I expected. If I had thought things were dire before, I realized that it was an understatement. A rather morbid one. People were actually dying.

Apparently, in this new timeline, Naira was the Defense Administrator of the entire Lunar Space Station. It was, in effect, a position equal to that of Vice president of North America, back when it was called the United States. She was one of the General's right hand people. At least, she should have been.

However, She had been given the control of the Lunar Interplanetary Administration's entire military force. This resource made it easy for her to begin an underground resistance to the General. Apparently, a journalist had begun to do some digging and started to expose her, when he was mysteriously killed.

At first, it had seemed like a coincidence, then other investigative journalists the public commonly viewed as "Conspiracy Theorists" started showing up dead or missing. Soon the Established Media broke from their monotonous newsworthy agenda and began to investigate the entire situation. They discovered that something huge was happening. Suddenly, reports about how Naira was trying to overthrow the General became widespread, with her being responsible for the death of many reporters, belonging to both Mainstream and Independent alike just for uncovering the truth.

When I was finally done reading the papers, I realized that I could see why dad and Zyra were having huge concerns. If Naira wasn't against killing, then she'd probably kill the General as well.

I was actually surprised that she hadn't done it just yet. Perhaps she was waiting for more popular support. Why? Most people on the Lunar Plane were against her. A lot of news articles were public outcries against her life and personality. The General, on the other hand, was beloved by the people, and every time an election came around, there were always votes in massive support for him.

I felt truly scared for Zyra, even as I folded the newspapers and dumped them on my reading table. For a long time that night, I stared at the ceiling, wondering what would have happened if I hadn't changed things. If I hadn't felt the need to prove dad wrong. If I...

Then I reminded myself that the what-ifs wouldn't change a thing. What had happened, happened. Now all I needed to do was figure out a way to explain things to Zyra and then help her sort all of this out. She could never be disloyal to the General, and she was the Chief of Staff, which meant she would be a prime target of Naira.

I needed to ensure that she was safe.

CHAPTER 10

1 - 2022

"The General disappeared."

When Zyra called me with the news, she sounded so terrified, I had to leave home immediately, wearing my flip-flops and pajamas.

On my way to hers, I tried to settle my thoughts, knowing I wouldn't be any good to her if I was also scared and worried when I got there. I began to think about how I told her what I did with the whole time-travel thing.

"Well, you were always the person to do the most outlandish things." Zyra complimented. "Not just your dress and grooming." She was referring to my Punk Rockish look. For me it didn't seem like an obsession or style I had for a while. There was this fleeting thought that I once had an interest in all things classical and medieval. Not anymore. When I asked Zyra about the details, she said I've always been a metal head. Dad took me to my first rock concert on Lunar Prime when I was 15.

Yet the strangest part of all of this "change" in me, I suppose, was my Quantum Chain. I was looking around for a gold necklace with a small port on it. Had I lost it? Maybe it was stolen? I dreaded that last thought. Suddenly, I forgot what I was looking for. Part of my fashion was a black, gold laced choker. I always kept it in my drawer. On the back of it was a small port—hmm... I swore that I never had this thing ever. It was then that it dawned on me—the Quantum Chain was always that fancy looking choker. Or was it? Eh, not important anymore.

That afternoon, she came to the house and we went straight up to my room. She had pizza. Zyra still hadn't lost her mother hen touch, and it didn't even matter what time period we were in. I was afraid of what she would say when I told her, just a little bit.

We talked for a very long time, and she kept asking me questions. She was a bit upset by the whole thing, and even looked sad at some point, when I told her that we used to be siblings instead of cousins. After a while though, she came around and told me that she understood my motives for doing all I did. She even asked to see the chain. I had been keeping it in a very safe place in my home, but when I found out about all that was going on with Naira and how the nation was soon going to go into a state of emergency, I began to wear it around my neck instead, beneath my shirt. When I brought it out and showed her, she looked shocked.

"Can we travel back in time right now?" she asked me, and I shook my head. I was so not doing that. "Come on, Sigma. It would be fun, going back in time and knowing things that other people don't. Don't tell me you wouldn't want that."

I shook my head, keeping my expression sober, even though I wanted to laugh at her antics. Zyra could be such a child at times. "It's not because it wouldn't be fun or anything like that, Zyra. But just think about the repercussions this time. Look what happened when I went into the past. The present changed, and it's so much worse than I could have ever imagined.

"Do you really want to take the risk of something like this happening all over again? I mean, really. What if things get even worse?"

I didn't mean to get so harsh, but my own guilt made me speak that way. When I saw her recoil a bit, I stretched out my hand and drew her to myself, hugging her stiff body until she relaxed and sighed. "I know you understand why I'm not doing this, Zyra. I know you do."

She nodded, her head nudging my neck, before she pulled back. "Yes, I do. If there's one thing I've learned, being Chief of Staff in this station wide unrest, it's that actions have consequences, and often really terrible ones. I can't imagine things being much worse than they already are, but I do see your point."

"Thanks, Z," I said.

When I pulled over at her house, the guards were standing right out front. I was expecting to maybe get asked for ID or something, but I guessed they were probably used to seeing me around here, so they let me in quite peacefully.

Zyra was sitting with her brother, her eyes red with all of the tears she'd already cried. Her mom was asleep on the couch, but even her face looked tear-streaked, so I figured she probably cried herself to sleep, exhausted from the emotional stress. Zyra rushed over to me as soon as I stepped in, throwing herself into my outstretched arms. I hugged her silently as she began to cry, not knowing what to say to console her.

I hugged William, her brother, once she let me go. Zyra began to tell me, slowly and hoarsely, how everything happened. Apparently, she had left the General in the office that afternoon when they had received a bomb threat in one of the biggest shopping malls on the Lunar Space Station.

They probably would never have taken it so seriously, but for everything else that had been going on recently. The General had been left with a few of his guards. By the time they discovered that the threat was just a sham, and nothing was going on, she came back to the office and he was gone.

Zyra kept shivering, but I knew it wasn't the cold. It was the fear and uncertainty, the terror of something bad happening to her father. I felt powerless, because there was nothing we could do but wait, try to find him. We began to search, but we didn't find any traces. None of the guards said a word, not even when they had all been imprisoned on the charge of treason.

The entire nation was wondering what was going to happen—what we would do? If Naira had really succeeded in taking out the General, then we knew that it would be only a short while before she accomplished the rest of her plan to take over the entire LSS.

We kept hoping, waiting for news that maybe the General had been found, or at the very worst, his body. We knew that the LSS couldn't be left without a leader for too much longer. In fact, there were already rumblings in the background that a few people wanted to go for the position.

We heard no word from Naira either. She had stopped actively participating in government for a long while, even on a surface level, but we knew that she had a lot to do with the underground businesses. Consequently, we weren't deluding herself that her apparent withdrawal meant she had given up on her plans.

On the 12th day of the month, Naira went on air. It was at some secret location, so we couldn't track her down. I left home for a long while to come stay with Zyra and offer her some support, and so we were together when my dad called me and told me to turn on the TV.

I asked him if there was a particular channel we were supposed to tune to, but he hung up before I could ask. While Zyra tried to call him back, I turned on the TV. We quickly realized why dad didn't tell us any channel in particular.

Across all the channels, they were showing Naira Hill-Adega

broadcasting her message on all channels. The woman didn't look like someone who would act so atrociously horrific as she'd been doing. But looks and personality can often deceive. At face value, she was petite, slim and small. Her eyes were a very light blue that looked like the sky approaching midday, and her hair was platinum blond. She was also quite striking, if not really beautiful. If one didn't know what was beneath her skin, they would think she was angel.

The broadcast repeated:

"This broadcast is just to let the entire Lunar Space Station know that I will now be taking over the reigns of the government. As General William Raylor Mellis has been out of office for months, I do not believe that it is out of place for another competent ruler to step up and take over the handling of our affairs.

I believe, as many, if not all of you do, that I am the right person to take up this responsibility. I have training on what goes on in the government, and as the former Defense Administrator I believe that all I have learned will serve to advance the Lunar Space Station.

I will be arriving at the capital to take over the position within the next few days, and I know that I will receive the maximum cooperation from the people." She paused. "Should any attempt to cause war or uprising within the nation, there will be swift retribution and grievous consequences."

After listening to it, I turned off the TV. So Naira thinks she can take over and think the people will accept her as the new leader of the Lunarian Society without a vote? Let's see how long that lasts!

CHAPTER 11

2 - 2022

It was as if what we had all been waiting for finally happened. The battle lines had been drawn, and it was time for us to pull out our swords. It wasn't as if any of us really wanted to rule the LSS, but we knew that Naira coming into power was going to be disastrous for all of us, and we couldn't allow her do what she wanted.

As soon as we realized that we couldn't trust the military anymore, we had to let the guards go. Some stayed but their loyalties were tested on a regular basis. We knew there were more drastic measures we had to take. Immediately, I told my dad that he needed to get any of his retired veteran friends, and anyone they trusted who had been staunchly against Naira coming into power to help us. We needed resources for new safe houses. All the current ones were deemed "compromised" Zyra would move into one of them there with her mom, my dad and I. William Jr. refused to come with us, saying he had his own plans. No one tried to persuade him, there wasn't really a point to that.

We knew we had to go into hiding before Naira's people could find us. We previously lived in Sector A, the Government district, because that was where the General worked. As Dean of Lunar University, William Jr. lived alone in Sector B, known as the Student District. Dad and I had lived in Sector C, the Residential District. The new safe houses were in a building within Sector D, the Industrial District. Those who lived here were factory workers and those who took care of the station's maintenance duties. Though this population was smaller than the others, they had the most important job of all-to keep the station running smoothly. Doing so kept us all alive.

It was the best place we could move to, because it was the one place where we felt we could hide. Just before we finalized the plans to get out, we discovered throughout some secret communication with William Jr. that Naira now had the complete support of the Police Force. Also, IT agents working for her installed secret cameras and identification software in various places around the station.

The day finally arrived, and we were able to transport the family to Sector D. It was a long and arduous travel, especially for Zyra's mom, who had never had it really hard in her life. Still, we pulled through, and moved to the house, which we were now going to be using as the headquarters of the resistance.

As soon as they had been transported, I went back home. I knew that we needed people to keep an eye on things, people to get information and make sure that the people who were distrustful of Naira would realize that there was still something left for them-hope.

It was lucky that we weren't the only group of people resisting Naira's reign. I figured that it was kind of like the hydra in those mythical stories-the many heads of a snake fighting against one legendary hero or group of adventurers. Perhaps if we could manage to distract her well enough, we would kill her and her supporters off and then be able to bring peace back to the LSS.

Saying it was easy though. As soon as I got back to the government Sector A, I knew that things weren't working out exactly as I'd expected. For one, people seemed to be scared to talk or even speak about Naira in public. The ones who criticized did so quietly, but most didn't.

All of the newspapers were now only carrying Naira approved articles. It was scary, how she'd managed to bend so many people to her side so fast. She had already taken the seat of power and was already making decrees and laws.

One of the first things she did was pronounce the General as dead, even though his body hadn't been found. She even organized a whole day of mourning for him. Not that anyone believed she was mourning though.

I had to go into hiding, not really sure about anyone at me. It was why I hadn't been able to make regular entries in my journal. I never knew that trying to avoid death or jail was this difficult, and I knew that those were the only fates that awaited me if I was to fall into Naira's hands, or those of her henchmen. I was too close to the General and to Zyra for her to feel comfortable leaving me alive.

Then one day, out of the blues, Zyra called me. We had agreed not to call unless it was very serious, just in case anyone was tracking conversations.

"Sigma, dad's here!" I couldn't help the loud gasp that escaped my lips when she told me that.

"But... But I thought..." I was stuttering unable to finish my thoughts or my words. Then she explained to me about how, though some of the men who surrounded him had been Naira's, there had been a few who still honored him and decided to help him escape to safety whenever they got the opportunity.

He had been in hiding in Sector D for a long time before us, but when he discovered that his family was also there, he'd decided to come out of hiding and go be with them. William Jr. knew where he was the whole time through secret communication channels only he and his son are authorized to use. Yet they were only to be used in case of emergencies. Neither knew that an insurrection would count as such.

I was so excited, I decided I might as well go on and travel back to see him. I figured it wasn't as if I was doing much good here, having to hide so much of the time.

I did my best to ensure that I settled everything I needed to before leaving. That morning, I booked my transport arrangements. I felt it was better, not giving anyone the opportunity to prepare to hurt me or something.

I was just on my way to the port where I would take the shuttle, when I was grabbed, yanked into an alley, and thrown violently against the ground, so hard I actually could feel my body bruise. When I opened my eyes, I saw two men. The biceps of the leaner one was probably just about the size of my torso. One of them was a dark-skinned man had silver short hair, wearing a brown overcoat. The other, his subordinate, referred to him as Lord Emmanuel.

They had to be Naira's men, probably part of the military. I believed it was the end for me. I always prided myself on being strong, on being able to fight back. But there was no point. I stayed there on the ground, staring up at them, hoping with the last of my strength that my family would survive the coming days.

The men were already approaching me, probably ready to kill. Lord Emmanuel took out a strange looking energy pistol and aimed it at me. Just as he pulled back on the trigger, then they came out of nowhere—three of them. I had to watch the most brutal fight I had ever seen, play out right before my very eyes.

Lord Emmanuel escaped with his life but his subordinate bit the dust. Then the woman of this group approached me with bloodstained hands and held one out to me. I felt kind of petty, groaning because of some cuts and bruises when she had just been in an actual fight. She led me out of the alley and I followed dumbly, the two men bringing up the rear. When we were out in the open, she turned to me. She spoke to me in a light middle-eastern accent.

"Hello. I'm Detective Zahra Melech." she then gestured at the man on my right. "With me are Detectives Othniel Goodman and Francis Karr." She gestured at the other guy on the opposite side of him near her. "We were here just in time to save you. In case you're wondering, William Jr. and the General had us follow you from afar for your protection."

I nodded gratefully, though the words would not leave my mouth because I was still in shock. Detective Goodman nodded to me in reply, then he ushered me onto the shuttle.

CHAPTER 12

3 - 2022

When I get home and everyone sees me, they try to treat me like an egg and things like that, but I'm not delicate. Instead, I spent time with the General, trying to find out everything about where he had been, what he had done, things like that.

He told me so many stories, some that made me laugh and some that brought tears to my eyes. At one point, I learned something that had tears running down my face. Apparently, there had been a time when he was unable to get food. The General had to scavenge for food that people had left to rot, and he even fell so sick, he could barely stand. Then he met Othniel, Zahra, and Francis. They noticed him trying to be incognito by dressing and acting like a homeless person just to evade Naira and her men. Yet Othniel was the first to know by his habits that he wasn't a true homeless person. Secretly following him, he learned how he was in contact with William Jr. through hidden access ports throughout the sector. The General knew Othniel and his team could be trusted because his entire family was such praiseworthy individuals. All of Othniel's family was in law enforcement and whole-hardheartedly supported the General in all his endeavors. When Naira began the purge, the Goodman family went into hiding and still are. Othniel was charged with the task to find and keep the General and his family safe. The others in the family only showed themselves when necessary. Zahra and Francis were co-workers who wanted to see this mission completed.

When the General was done telling me all of that, he looked so unburdened. I knew he would never have been able to tell his family, partly because of pride and also because he didn't want them to carry the weight of knowing how much trouble he had faced.

Still, we were all so grateful that he was alive, and he was fine. We also knew that there was problem with us remaining in this place. Naira's agents were appearing more frequently here, and we knew that they would soon discover us if care was not taken.

Zyra and I began to develop plans to transport our parents, as well as some of their other relatives and administrators who remained loyal to the General, to one of the Lunar Colonies on the moon below. Finally, we decided on Lunar-2, and began to set the wheels in motion.

It made things very difficult, the fact that we couldn't just speak to anyone, but we had to be very selective in the people we brought in on the decision making process. In the end, those who we chose undoubted believed Naira was unfit to rule.

We finally were able to find a shuttle, and we started making contact with people from Lunar-2. It was the easiest part of the process, because they also knew Naira to be a false prophet and a hypocrite, so they were ready to render their help. Plus, the General helped them rebuild after a catastrophic incident had left most of their environment destroyed. Zyra and I were working overtime, trying to ready everything. We knew how just one flaw in an otherwise perfect plan could destroy everything we were doing, and we didn't want that.

Naira was still continuing her threats. She was really advancing in her bid to seize total control of everything in the nation. Weekly raids were being carried out on the Government, Student, and Residential Sectors. If any household or person was found with items that were termed treasonous, they were swiftly and unmercifully punished. Currently, she didn't have the manpower to do raids in the Industrial sector yet. That was a relief but we all knew this setback was temporary. Through it all, we could still hear of men who wanted to wrest control of the government from Naira. We hoped all of it was keeping her busy while we finished up our business here.

I hadn't known of Zyra's plans until the day when I was supposed to bid them farewell. The previous night, we had a huge family/friends dinner, shared stories and just talked for a while. Zyra had spoken to everyone privately, and I knew she was trying to reassure them and herself that things would still turn out fine.

I didn't realize until later that she slipped out of the house with Othniel, Zahra, and Francis. It was the next morning, when everyone was already boarding the shuttle that we realized that Zyra and the other three were nowhere to be found.

Scared, the others and I began to try and call her, but we received no answer. We couldn't delay the transport much longer in order not to draw too much unwanted attention, I decided that they should get on the shuttle and leave, and that once I found Zyra, I would communicate with them. It was the worst decision of my life, even worse than the decision to create something that could change time.

Barely seconds after the shuttle took off I received an encoded message from Zyra on my phone. Usually, she typed well, her words perfectly crafted.

"SHUTTLE BOMB" the message read.

I got her message pretty clearly.

At once, I began to wave my hands at the shuttle, trying to get the pilot's attention. Only, they were too far, and they could not see me. I watched them go farther, farther. I began to hope that maybe, just maybe, Zyra's text had been mistaken. Maybe I had read her wrong.

Then it happened, so fast, yet my mind took in the details and I knew, even then, that I was going to remember it forever. I watched the shuttle explode, watched as pieces of it began to rain down. I didn't know that I was running, didn't realize that I was crying, that my heart was breaking in two.

I almost didn't hear the squeal of the car behind me, but I did, and when I looked, it was Zyra. She waited for me to come in and sit with her, and then she drove us closer and closer.

I could feel my breath catch in my hands, and my breath hurt with the effort it took to control myself. When we got to the scene, we both knew that there was no one inside it who could have survived. And so we clung to each other, holding on and crying and consoling and trying to tell ourselves that it was going to be alright when we weren't even sure anything was going to be alright.

We waited while some of the commercial district police officers came over and checked through. They told us it had to be a bomb, and that they were sorry. As if sorry could heal. As if sorry could bring them back.

It was the worst day of my life, and even now, as I write, I cannot help the tears that flow down my face, wetting my tablet's screen. I sometimes wonder if the wounds left on my heart from watching most of my family die in a single incident would ever heal.

CHAPTER 13

4 - 2022

It was only later, when Zyra and I left the scene of the incident that she broke down in tears, "I didn't want to let anyone see it. I got this just as I was arriving here. Then I forwarded it to you because I was so scared. I thought...oh, this is all my fault. I should have been there. I should have traveled with them, but I was so strong-headed. I wanted to stay here and fight."

She continued to cry, losing her focus on the road, swerving. She pulled over at the curb. I knew that it wasn't safe for her to drive for the time being so we traded places. We sat there crying in each other's arms.

"Please don't think like that, Zyra," I choked out when I could actually speak out of my own grief. "If you were gone, I wouldn't be sane. You can't think like that, okay? We have only each other now, and we have to live with it."

She nodded, her hair tickling me and making me giggle. I wondered how I could laugh right then, but I couldn't stop. Then Zyra also began to laugh, and we both giggled there together for a long while, before the tears began to fall again. Exhausted, we drove back to the home where we had stayed in with our family, enjoying so much love and friendship.

Now, we knew we had to leave. We couldn't go back here because now that the police here knew our address—we'd had to give it to them when we gave our statements, and we hadn't exactly been thinking clearly. So we packed up everything left in the house that would be traced to us, and then we got out of the place.

Zyra and I talked a lot during the road trip, trying to make plans on how exactly we were going to combat the evil force of Naira, now that it seemed like it was just us two left. Zyra was of the opinion that we needed to infiltrate the ranks. I told her that I felt it was dangerous, but she reminded me of the people who saved me in that alley, telling me that if there were people who could do that, then there certainly were people who would be able to help us.

She started going out in public again but changed her features a little so that it wouldn't be very obvious who she was. I was scared for her, but she had become even more reckless since we lost our families, and I couldn't hold her back.

Then one day, she came home shivering, staring at me in shock when I opened the door for her.

"Hey, what is it?" I asked her, pulling her into the house and shutting the door. When she was still shivering after a few seconds despite the fact that it wasn't a very cold day, I finally had to get her out of her clothes so I could hug her to myself and just wait for her to come out of whatever place she had gone to. It was minutes later before she began to speak.

"I almost died." Her voice came out so shaky, I couldn't at first comprehend the words. Through an only extraordinary feat of self control made me not jump up and begin to yell at her."

"What do you mean you almost died?" I asked, as calmly as I could manage. Then I listened to her explain how she has been going out as usual, listening in for those rare conversations that would make her guess that maybe a particular person wasn't really as loyal to Naira as they should.

Then she would try to speak with them, confirm all other details, and then store that. She planned to recruit as many people as possible.

She told me how she'd approached two men she heard speaking derogatorily about Naira, and it turned out out to be a trap to lure her and kill her.

Then out of nowhere, a woman appeared and rescued her. The woman introduced herself as Val, and she also asked why Zyra hadn't seen the message in time to save her family.

"That was her not you?" I asked, surprised. Zyra nodded. "So where is this Val woman now and where did she leave you?"

"She brought me all the way here and then just kind of disappeared around the corner or something in a flash of light.

We tried for a long time to try to determine Val's identity, but Zyra hadn't been able to identify her voice or her face or anything else that could help them determine who she was. At the end, they decided to stop and just concentrate on being grateful that Zyra was alive and well.

Of course, things got even worse after that. Naira somehow managed to discover our hideout, and then she got my face on the news. I became the Chief Enemy on the State. It meant that if I was ever found, I was to be captured at any cost, even death. However, the most annoying of it all was the name she gave me, "Doctor Chronos". Like I'm some kind of timekeeper. Everyone knew about my research on time-travel but Naira seemed to believe in her Media "Hit Pieces" about me say that her setbacks were attributed to me and my time traveling friends from the future. She deemed the tech we use as "DE'MS", her slang term for demonic, reasoning that only God should have the power to manipulate time. Each article always referred to me as "the So Called Doctor of Time, Dr. Time Herself, or Doctor Chronos". What's also new was that these articles quoting her in anything called her Queen Adega. Her vanity and hypocrisy dumbfounded me.

Most if not all hit pieces about me talked about me owning a technological device of evil that could destroy our world. I knew she was talking about the Quantum Chain, because time-travel is the only thing that could threaten her reign. I could barely go out now, because whenever I did, people wanted to capture or kill me. From what Zyra reported, there was even a bounty on my head, and who wouldn't want to win something like that? I was so scared of how dangerous things were, I decided to start working on jumping time again. Perhaps, if I was able to go back in time, I would be able to change some things and not allow the future be so terrible.

When I told Zyra, she looked so excited. "I want to go with you." she said, and I shook my head.

"I do not think I can take you with me, Z. I think it can only take one. But don't worry, I'll make one of your own for you. Is that fine?"

She pouted a little, but then she finally just shrugged and gave in. "Do what you have to do, Sigma," she said, hugging me one last time before she stepped away.

I set the clock, paused to take in a deep breath, and then set it. The last thing I saw was Zyra's teary face.

CHAPTER 14

5 - 2027

I immediately knew something was wrong when I made the time jump. This wasn't the past, it couldn't be. I looked around, and everywhere looked so unfamiliar, and not in a good way. It felt as if the entire place had been deserted.

I couldn't see anyone outside. There were no plants, nothing to show life but the few buildings scattered around. I wasn't even sure where I was, except for the fact that I was standing at someone's doorstep. Not wanting to be caught by anyone who was perhaps working for Naira or whatever evil dictator was ruling right now, I started to walk away, then the door opened.

"Sigma!" The voice was familiar, and I turned. "What the heck are you doing out here? Why didn't you just knock? Come on in." It was Othniel. Relieved, I smiled and ducked beneath his giant arm to walk into the living room. Nina and Terrel were both standing in there, and they both hugged me when I walked in.

"Hey, how are you guys doing?" I asked, pulling off my jacket. "How have things been?" I didn't really hear much of their reply, because I could see the hologram calendar on the wall. 2027. Do I was right. I hadn't gone back, I had gone into the future. I couldn't continue doing this, making mistakes and being unsure about the place I was going to end up. I needed to somehow refine the Quantum Chain, make it as foolproof as possible, as soon as I can. Turning back to the room, I tuned in to the conversation.

"How has the resistance been going?" I asked, settling into the couch. They all did the same. The place, small as it was, was quite comfortable. They had made the little building into a home, and she loved it. The walls were a light blue shade that made it look more spacious, and though the curtains were drawn, rays of sunlight still shone through.

There weren't any pictures on the walls though. Whoever decorated this place was kind of a minimalist, and I guessed why. Whenever they were attacked by Naira's people, they wanted to be able to travel as light and move as fast as they could.

A lady in feminine martial artist attire spoke. Nina Goodman, Othniel one and only sister. She started off with answering my question. "It's been really..." she gave a deep sigh, and rolled her neck from side to side. "It's been really tough, you know. I mean, you do know."

"We are like the last of the lot, the last ones still standing against Naira's rule. It feels like she has either taken everyone to her side, or killed the ones that wouldn't yield. Only a few days ago, they got a few of us, members of the Initiative, I mean, in jail, and we've been trying to find where they are so we'll be able to bust them out. It's been really rough though," Terrell said. Terrell Espinoza was a distant relative, black man of Hispanic decent. He was the Initiative's top spy.

We were all quiet for a while as we thought of the ones who had died, who had been jailed or else just disappeared. I know they felt as if had been struggling so hard for so long, and it seemed like they were barely accomplishing anything. I could relate actually, though I hadn't been through exactly what they had. Nina began to talk to me about her experience with Othelius, her and Othniel's cousin, as break-dancers.

"It's been our cover, actually. We are allowed to go to a lot of places we would not really get into if they didn't think we were merely there for entertainment purposes. It helps us to listen in on conversations—you know, discover secrets and stuff like that. The soldiers and enforcers are usually very loose lipped when they think that no one is really paying attention, and so it's very easy.

"Then we relate the information to the rest of the Initiative. We can make use of what part of the information is useful to us. Especially when it comes to things like raids."

Terrell stood close to the window, an energy pistol in his hand. I figured they probably needed to stand guard at all times so that they wouldn't be caught unawares if Naira's soldiers came.

Othniel came in from wherever he and his team of three went, bringing drinks. "We do not usually get to have such luxuries, but once in a while I figure we need to let loose. Your presence gives us opportunity to do that."

"So how has it been for you, Othniel?" I asked as he poured the drinks. It was just soda, but it felt like a mix of some exotic wine, with how rare such pleasures were these days.

"Family Life, the Initiative, or the government?" he sounded confused.

"Any? All? I asked in reply, and he shook his head. He went over to hand Terrell a drink, then came back to sit with Nina and I.

"This new Monarchy has been pretty terrible, but them everyone knows that. There isn't much to say about it, other than that we are really hoping there is a break soon. We need some help, because people are giving up already."

“We have all the help we need from Dr. Time Herself.” Othelius said in his raspy voice. His words had a tone of confidence in them. As if he believed the rumors about my Quantum Chain.

“If could work on making the Quantum Chain more stable, I would be able to send more people back in time. Maybe that would stabilize things. I needed time to think, time to plan, time to work.” I told them.

Everyone around me believed that with the right resources, making the Quantum Chain more stable could be done. They all revered me to be this “hero” but I don't think I've accomplished anything good with time-travel now. If anything, the problems I believed to have fixed with it ended up creating another one. Time is broken and I'm the girl who broke it!

I felt that my greatest invention was also my greatest failure, messing with laws of nature that didn't just affect me but everyone that existed. I just wished this was all some kind of nightmare I could wake up from. That would be some dream to be this long! I knew this was my new reality. I can't say it was a total loss. I've gained friends and allies I didn't have in the previous timeline like the Initiative. They're my family as well as Zyra. All of them have faith in my tech and I should too. Knowing such made me feel a little better.

CHAPTER 15

6 - 2027

Over the next few weeks, I learned a lot more about how they were operating. Terrell had a background in the military. He was a soldier. When the purge happened, Terrell became the Initiative's eyes and ears of what was going on within the Monarchy. He still had a small network of others like him throughout the Queen's army. They were those who didn't really support her cause. However, they chose to remain in the army and delayed her plans if t meant killing innocents. Most of the time, these "moles" were found and executed.

Terrell did most of the heavy lifting by his own experience. With his people on the inside dying by the dozens every day, he knew eventually it would be hard for him to maintain his cover. He'd been able to get intelligence, and even some weapons in his last supply run. This gave us an edge, knowing that it would be very difficult for information to get to us because being discovered meant certain doom. Nina told me that in the entertainment world, she was known as Empress Catalina, while Othelius was called the Caesar. They were also helping the Initiative get a lot more money than they would usually expect to have with their winning dance battle competitions.

The little house they lived in, minimal as it was, I later found out was the command center of all operations. In the kitchen, there was a rather sophisticated communication center that only the three of them who lived there could access. No one would have easily discovered it. Until switched on by specific voice command, it looked to be just normal kitchen cabinetry. It was what they used in reaching out to the others who were loyal to the Initiative.

I also learned about the United Mercenary Organization of the Terran Elite, the secret organization that Queen Adega was using to carry out her nefarious plans. Head of it was a silver short haired man named Lord Emmanuel. Yet this one seemed a bit older than the one that I encountered. He had a scar on his face like he was suffering from Lupus or something similar.

According to Nina, Othelius and Terrell, UMOTE was underground for a very long time, until some brave journalist decided to infiltrate them in 2025. That led to UMOTE's exposure to the rest of the Lunar Space Station. A few days later, the journalist was killed in a freak flying accident, but the uproar they raised led to the recruitment of more members into the Initiative. Unfortunately, when UMOTE became exposed, instead of continuing to operate in the shadows, they had their Queen's blessing to act as her “Assassination Squad” to stamp out all rebels.

Nina told her about some experiences she'd heard people had in the hands of these men. Apparently, one of the ladies who recently joined in had been an ardent supporter for a very long time of Queen Adega. Apparently, that was how Naira still wanted to be addressed-until UMOTE agents killed her entire family, based on a blog post her cousin wrote as satire against the Queen.

The young woman also provided a very good source of information, because her previous circles did not know about her current affiliation with the Initiative, so they were still willing to gossip with her about a lot of things, which made her a good source.

I began to learn the Initiative's mode of operations, helped them keep guard and other duties that needed attention. Within days, they were all looking healthier, as they had had more sleep and time to do other things.

We sent word across to where Zyra is that I'm here already, and they send back a message that she would be coming over to visit very soon.

That seems to perk Nina, Othelius and Terrell up like nothing else since I had been here, so I asked them why they were so excited. "I just so love her!" Nina exclaimed as she smiled widely. "Zyra is so wonderful. She's kind, and she takes time out of her busy schedule to visit once in a while. She knows how to engage you in a conversation, you know."

Othelius nodded earnestly. "When Nina and I told her we were going to be break dancers, she went to get books on the topic and then she studied it so we would be able to talk. She even showed us a few new techniques in the books that are working really well for us right now."

"Hey," Terrell said, "do you know why she hasn't decided to run against Naira and Win the elections?"

"Yeah, I've been thinking about it for a while," Nina said, standing up and walking around the room, like someone who had a lot of energy and nowhere to put it. "I mean, she has the support of almost the entire LSS, so if she runs against Naira, she'll certainly win."

"I told you guys that she probably has a very good reason, and you didn't need to keep thinking about it," Terrell said sternly, and they both glanced at him.

"Yeah," Nina said quietly. "Sorry. I guess we were just too curious about stuff, and we should just be patient and trust that she has a plan."

Othelius nodded in agreement. I couldn't stop the thought from playing over in my mind though, was I waited for Zyra to show up. If she was going to get popular support, then why hadn't she run? I couldn't help but stare at Terrell, who was over by the window, watching.

It seemed like he knew a lot more about Zyra than he was saying. That was something else I needed to ask. Yes, there were matters of life and death, of the continued prosperity of the LSS or its gradual destruction.

But there was nothing as fun as heckling Zyra until she shared some things with me. And heckle I would, as soon as she got here.

CHAPTER 16

7 - 2027

When Zyra saw me, she threw herself at me. At once, we went off into another room to talk. And we did have a lot to talk about. "So, the Initiative, huh?" I asked with a smirk.

She winced. "I first opted for the Raylorian Initiative but our mission isn't just about us."

"I know, I know," I replied, this time laughing. She hugged me again. "I've missed you so much. Welcome back. So, I guess the others would have told you a little about the things that have been happening, of course."

"Yes, they have," I replied. Someone knocked on the door. It was Nina, and she held an aluminum tray in her hands, bearing a jug of coffee, two cups, and then an assortment of other things that would probably be added to the drink.

"I come bearing gifts," she said with a smile. "You guys have a nice time, and if you need anything, just ask, okay?" She said.

We both nodded, and then Zyra went to pour the coffee. "So I guess since you are probably up to speed about everything in general, you'd want to ask about me specifically."

"I do so love how you always cut straight to the point, Z," I said with a small smile, receiving the cup from her and taking a seat on one of the chairs in the room. She sat on the other and we both stared at each other for a while.

"So..."

"So..."

At our simultaneous speech, we both began to laugh. "Alright, enough of that," she said. "What do you want to know?"

"Well, I think the obvious, actually. According to what I've been told, you have the popular support of the people, just like the General once did. So it's actually surprising that you haven't taken up the reins of the country's affairs.

"I mean," I added when she smiled. Sometimes I forgot that she was a lot older than me in this timeline. All of my time traveling was already making me lose my memory. Shaking my head at that thought, I continued, "Five years ago it was kind of understandable, you know. We were afraid for our lives and running away from everyone. But now, things are more settled.

She looked lost in thought for a very long time. With a heavy sigh, she focused her attention on me again. "You'd think that things are easier, mow that I have the support of the people, but it's actually the other way round. Do you remember Val?"

The name sounded familiar, and then it clicked. "She once rescued you from being killed, right? I remember."

"Yes, that's Val. Well..." Unaware of it, Zyra was tugging out a loose strand from her dress and twining it around her finger. "She"s from the future."

I froze when she uttered those words. To think that someone else perfected my technology from the future. What's more—they knew the exact moment when things were going south then used that knowledge to change the past!

“She told me everything that was going on behind the scenes but the unfortunate change was the shuttle incident.” Zyra's tone dropped. “She believed someone from her timeline planted the bomb.”

"What do you mean?"

“Checking the evidence, Val said that the explosive device used hadn't been invented yet.”

Then I thought about that older looking man with the silver hair and facial scar.

“And you know why I never ran against Naira?”

“Lemme guess, Val told you not to?”

"Correct!" Zyra answered. "Well, you know we have the midterm elections, and the people are supposed to vote and the most popular candidate will definitely win. Do you think no one has run against Naira in the two times since we've had these elections?"

Comprehension began to dawn on me as I listened. "You mean...the people who have run against her are dead. I mean, it's not like we have a body or something, but I figure the fact that they have disappeared and no one has seen them since then speaks for itself, doesn't it?"

"Yes, it does. It really does." I shook my head as I sipped my tea. It wasn't normal, the amount of greed Naira had, and how power hungry she was.

"Val was the one who brought all of the weaponry and some of the other stuff, the ones that Terrell had not been able to get. She told me about what UMOTE stood for—The United Mercenary Organization of the Terran Elite. And those guys are terrible. They're the reason why Naira's so powerful. No one can run against her unless they have a death wish!"

I watched Zyra shiver. "Yes, Nina told me a few things about them and the atrocities they have been committing." I replied. Zyra stood up and went to look out through the window.

"They have successfully made everyone who could take that position and do something meaningful with it either disappear or die or something. I'm not really interested in a date such as that," she said. Her arms were still folded around herself, and I studied Zyra once more, seeing things I hadn't noticed on my first, more casual glance.

She was slimmer now, and though there was strength in her carriage, there was also fragility, a sense of brittleness that told me she was barely holding herself together.

"Zyra? Come over here," I called to her. I couldn't keep the concern out of my tone. "How are you doing?" I asked. I wondered if anyone thought to ask her that these days. Maybe they just assumed she was fine.

She smiled at me. "I'm... oh, Sigma. I feel like I'm so lost. No family, no real friends...I mean, I am grateful for the Initiative and everyone who is here, but I'm kind of just apart, you know. Alone. More like a symbol than an actual person. And that's difficult for me."

I took her hand and held it between both of mine. "I know it's hard, and it feels like you are alone. But you are not. These people out there, they care. They love you. I saw them speak about you, and you are more than a symbol. You are a friend, family even."

And then I smiled, because tears were already beginning to drop from her eyes. "And now you have me. I'm here now. It's going to be fine, okay?"

She nodded, her grin widening through her tears. "Yes, okay."

CHAPTER 17

8 - 2027

I began to formulate a plan of attack for how we were going to bring Naira down once and for all.

I knew we were going to have to fight her UMOTE sooner or later. A mole told them where they believed our HQ was. A few UMOTE agents tried to get in. That's when we knew our time was limited. Our numbers shrunk by the day. I had been doing some calculations, and I figured we needed a few people to do it. I wasn't sure if I was going to be one of them, but now we had trustworthy people around, and I knew they could get the job done.

I started meeting more of the members of the Initiative as the entire organization planned to do an assault on Naira's stronghold in Sector A. We weren't as many as we used to be five years ago, but the few who were left persevered no matter the cost, and they were all the more stronger for it.

I started spending more of my time in the small space that had been sectioned off for me as a lab. I did not have all of my previous equipment, and it was a bit difficult procuring some of the things I needed, but somehow we managed to find most of it. The rest, I either did without, or if it was absolutely necessary, found something to use as a replacement. There was something else happening though. It seemed as if Naira had killed of every other facet or group that was standing against her, and she was now coming to meet us for the final battle.

We began to see more of her military in Sector D, when usually they were restricted to the other three Sectors. Realizing that we were under surveillance, we began to limit our movements, trying to be less exposed so that we would not provide them easy targets.

But they didn't wait for us to fight. One morning, Terrell woke us up with a sharp whistle. He had been making everyone in the entire compound of the Initiative headquarters to do drills, so that we would know what do in almost any scenario. He trained us to recognize any signal and the particular message he was sending.

So when we heard the whistle, we knew what he was trying to tell us.

Attack!

I think everyone at first panicked. Most of the ladies who were unmarried stayed together in two rooms. Zyra had told me I could have a bedroom all to myself, but I didn't feel comfortable with it. I was already using a private space as a lab, and that was enough.

After a few seconds though, we recalled our training and began to follow the steps that Terrell had taught us. Soon, we had all of the children and more vulnerable women shut up in the underground bunkers, where two of the men stood guard. Then the women who had been trained in battle headed down.

Some of us had learned how to shoot with the makeshift bows and arrows that we made from whatever scrap materials we found. We headed up to the protective roofs that had tiny holes through which we could shoot and joined the battle.

By the time the fighting was over, it had been hours, and it was almost done.

We headed down to take stock of what we had lost, injuries and fatalities. There were two men lying dead on the front of our property, where we had fought. A few others, including some women, had been deeply wounded. The ones among us that had medical training immediately started caring for them, with the women who had been left in the bunkers.

"Where is Terrell?" It was Zyra. I didn't think many would notice, but I could hear panic in her voice, fear. Could it be that I had misread the signs after all? Maybe there was a third reason why she had never acknowledged his feelings. "Where is Terrell?" She asked again.

But he wasn't there. And even before someone yelled, "And Nina," I already realized that she wasn't here either. Neither was Othelius. All three of them were gone.

CHAPTER 18

9 - 2027

We began to search for them, wanting to know where they were hidden or being kept, so that we would be able to prepare a plan of attack and break them out.

I also made sure I was there for Zyra. I didn't want to push her to share her feelings about Terrell with me, but I always made sure to be there with her, to let her know I was available if she needed to talk.

Coupled with my work in the lab and then being a lookout once in a while, I was stretched pretty thin. We all were, so I couldn't actually complain.

I didn't know that there were other members of the resistance who I hadn't met until the day that a truck arrived, bringing about eight people. When the last two came out, and then I got a good glimpse of the driver, I couldn't help my mouth dropping open.

I hadn't forgotten any of the three of them, not now and not since they saved my life. Zahra looked almost the same, except that her hair now had streaks of gray in it, and she looked slimmer. When our eyes met, she smiled.

I hadn't laughed as hard as I did then in a while. I ran towards her and threw my arms around her for a hug. "Oh, Zahra. I can't believe I'm meeting you again!"

She hugged me tight, and then released me. "You look good, honey. Glad to see that my effort in keeping you alive wasn't wasted." I laughed again. We hadn't exactly spoken that day when she save my life, but I already knew we were going to be very close friends.

Detective Goodman had been the last one to come out of the truck, and I held out my hand to him. "I never really thanked you for that day, detective. So glad I'm getting the chance right now."

He smiled, and the wrinkles in the corners of his eyes deepened. His crowfeet made him look distinguished. Just like Zahra, he had a lot more gray in his hair.

"And just as Zahra said, thank you for keeping yourself safe since then." Othniel moved past me smoothly and walked towards Zyra and Zahra. Yeah, weird, I know. Where he stopped, he and Zyra moved a few meters away and got into deep conversation, while Zahra walked into the building.

"I guess I don't earn a greeting then?" The voice from behind me startled me, making me jump really high. "Hey, hey, calm down."

I finally turned. It was Francis, and I should have guessed it was him. I mean, he did drive the truck here. The first time we met though, he'd said barely a word to me, and I figured he was really quiet. Maybe I was wrong.

"I'm sorry for startling you," he said, and I realized I had been staring dumbly at him for a while.

"Oh no, no. And I really should have thanked you, Francis." I held out my hand to him, and he looked down at it without expression. Wondering if maybe I had offended him, I started to pull it back and apologize when he took it with his own...no, hand is kind of an understatement. It was more like a paw, bigger than any human palm I'd ever seen before. I smiled at him, then gestured him in. He gazed at me for another long minute, before he nodded and went in.

An hour later, a few of us were called into a meeting, and Othniel addressed us. They had discovered where the others were. Nina, Othniel and Terrell were captured during the battle. We gathered a small network of humans and AIs to go rescue them. They would be leaving tomorrow morning, so that they would be able to meet, and then go on the attack. We all sent our good wishes with them, and I desperately hoped that Terrell especially was okay. Not that I didn't like the other two, but I didn't think Zyra would be able to take it if they didn't find him alive. He was our best man on the inside. Many believed that without him, we couldn't have gotten this far but losing him would be ever so more painful. I had some news of my own, as well as a discussion with Zyra I needed to have, but I knew it all had to be paused until they had done this.

It took all of us to persuade her to stay behind while the others went on the mission. I knew the only reason why we won that battle was because she remembered the last time people tried to persuade her to do something and she decided to do her own thing. She would probably never absolve herself fully of the blame for our families' death.

We waited all through the next day, just there watching, waiting, hoping, praying, afraid but holding on.

There was no communication at all, not that morning, not that evening, not the next morning and evening, and not the next. It was the evening of the fourth day when we heard the sound of a truck pulling into the compound.

The moment Othelius stepped out of the truck, the entire place roared in joy.

CHAPTER 19

10 - 2027

It took hours before we settled down to even hear the details of the recovery. Apparently, they had. Already gone in, not knowing that they were entering a trap. Then just as they were about to get attacked by some of the jailers and the military people in charge of that prison, Val had arrived. With her help, they had been able to fight off everyone and get out of there alive. Yet Othelius had a personal vendetta against the Queen. He believed her mistake was having them sent to a holding cell in the heart of her stronghold. Since the last attack on it was unsuccessful, the only way in was to get captured. The only problem was that one of them would have to stay behind.

That person was Terrell. They said he had a bomb strapped to him. Before the Queen's soldiers knew what was up, Terrell detonated himself. Out of the rubble was found several dozen bodies. Among them was Naira herself.

According to Zahra, as soon as Ohelius and Nina got out safely, Val cleared a path for Terrell to find the Queen on the inside. Some said he was gunned down before reaching her quarters.

“The stories are conflicting.” I said as the men that escaped with Othelius and Nina relayed to the group what went down during the rescue. Then I remembered what Zyra told me about Val. Maybe the bomb Terrell had on him was one she designed with future tech? In the rubble of Queen Adega's stronghold were traces of unidentified bomb fragments. When I looked over it, something screamed “futuristic”.

After a while though, I walked through the main hallway, Understanding my signal, Zyra followed me in immediately. I led the way to my lab, shutting the door as soon as we were both inside.

"So, I have been thinking. I told you I was working on something in my lab, and as soon as I was done, I would let you know." She nodded for me to continue. "I have been trying to build more of these." I tugged out my Quantum Chain from beneath my blouse.

Her eyes widened. "What? How...?"

"I had to scavenge for a lot things, but I do believe that I have fine-tuned the whole process. I wanted to develop it to the extent that you would be able to choose the exact day, time and place you would appear in, so that freak incidents like mine wouldn't be happening."

Her shock slowly changed to admiration. "You're amazing, Sigma. So how far have you gone? Do you need more items or—"

"Oh no. It was easier this time around, because I have my flash drive with me every time, and I already know what works. I just needed to find the parts. Nina and Othelius really helped out with that."

"Wow. So do you have something in mind?" She asked. I nodded. Quickly, I outlined my plan to her. She hummed. "Sounds very wonderful actually. But do you know who you want to carry it out?"

"I considered Nina and Othelius." I could see her sharp recoil, even though she tried to mask it with a cough. I didn't call her out on it though, or leave her to suffer long. "But then I changed my mind."

Acting as if I didn't hear her sigh of relief, I added, "I think Othniel, Zahra and Francis would work out really well. We should tell them together, as soon as possible."

She nodded. "Let's give them today to be happy. We'll call them in the evening to let them know the details of everything. You do realize that we cannot force them, don't you? It's one of the rules of the Initiative. We don't make people do what they don't want to do."

"I get that. We will ask them. Something tells me they would be more than willing though." They didn't seem like a team that loved to have too much downtime.

The next evening, we did just that. Once they were all settled, or at least sitting, because they seemed to be on the alert for an attack or something, Zyra started.

I could see Othniel's thoughtful gaze, Zahra's ready one, and Francis' undecipherable stare. When we finally presented the plan to them, Othniel had a lot of questions. I knew they were just that though, questions. They were totally into the whole idea. Especially if it meant we could stop Naira from completely taking over the Lunar Space Station.

As soon as they all finally agreed and said they were willing to go on the mission, I went for the small vault where I had been keeping the items. There were three, wrapped separately. I first explained the whole concept of how it worked, how they could set the time, date and place.

I made sure to explain it over and over, so they wouldn't forget. Finally, I handed over the items. Othniel's was a bracelet, and what I made for Francis was a ring. Zahra got the pendant.

Zyra asked if they understood the mission, then they went into to tell the others that they had another assignment and needed to leave. Then we took the truck to a more remote location, where they all did as I instructed. Then they vanished.

CHAPTER 20

11 - 2027

It's been a month since the end of the Queen's reign and we're already ahead of schedule on the reconstruction of our space station. Sector A was worked on first. The Initiative rebuilt Town Hall. Zyra quickly moved from the current safe house to there. Morale among the troops were higher than usual. Suddenly, towards the end of the month, Othniel and his team returned. And did they have a story to tell!

My head was spinning from not just the confusing timeline differences but from the euphoria of knowing the mission was a success. Let's start with the first one.

Detective Goodman, Melech, and Karr ran into their doppelgangers while there. In that world, time-travel made their alternative reality selves quite the time-traveling heroes. What's more, they belong to an organization known as the Time Travelers Administration. Detective Goodman said that in TTA, they all chose code names. 2kReturner is what Othniel Goodman chose. The Forest Flower was what Zahra was known as. Francis Karr chose Biz-R. Other difference was between the two Goodmans. Our Othniel's middle name was Silas but 2kReturner's was James.

Now onto the other me. The called her Dr. Time and the Time Guru alternately. Stop right there. I kinda figured I was stepping on someone's toes when I wanted to choose those aforementioned names as my moniker. Well, I guess Doctor Chronos was the better sounding of those options, even if its what the public already knew me as. It was either that or the Chronobreaker. Then again, that sounded off too. Based on the guilt I felt, Sigma the Chronobreaker wasn't such a bad nickname. Saying it out loud made me look crazy, meriting laughs and odd looks from around the room when I did. Doctor Chronos was a name far superior to the aforementioned. Anyway, Dr. Time, with the help of that timeline's General Mellis, founded TTA.

At first, Dr. Time invented time-travel as a project to test her limits as a Quantum Physicist but when the insurrection happened in winter 2024, that all changed. These events were related to the Evanston Massacre on Earth in 2021. UMOTE had a hand in killing the entire family before attempting to kill ours in that Timeline? Why? Cuz Naira believed they were unfit to live. Me personally, if that timeline's Naira was as much as a hypocrite as ours was, the Evanstons probably found some dirt on her or key family members that would've destroyed their reputation.

Detective Goodman mentioned that there was an aristocratic economic war going on when they first got there. The destination year was autumn 2021, 3 months before things went south in our timeline. I then realized that traveling that far into the past created a new timeline. Ours was set in stone by the Creator. There was no changing its past.

In this new timeline were three rich families dwelling on the Space Station: The Mellis', Hill-Adegas and the Evans-Pyuns. Two Lunarian University students, one from the Evans Family named Conner Evans fell for a trap that led to him and his future wife, Michelle Pyun, getting exiled from the lunar plane and forced to live on Earth. What trap was that? It was said Michelle was a loose woman. Asa Ravenscraft was her other boyfriend that lived with her and Conner in Sector B. Jail-time for breaking the "no shack up" law didn't phase them. Unfortunately, all aristocratic families had some sort of immunity to this kind of thing. The Hill-Adegas were hellbent on taking this family off the board. First, Asa went missing and his body was never found. Then Naira's cousins fabricated evidence against Conner, making backyard deals with a several terrorist organization on Earth, selling propriety technology to them. After the two's exile, the rest of their family protested by closing up shop and going elsewhere on Earth, leaving the lunar plane in mass. Unbeknownst to them all, they were vulnerable to UMOTE and their cronies who ruled a terrorist controlled planet. Changing his surname to the unimaginative Evanston one was not going to spare him from the fate that would soon befall his family, including his in-laws.

News about the Massacre was quickly hushed and those who dug further into the "whodunit" were found dead or never found at all. That was until TTA was formed in 2022. The General had his suspicions about Naira's shady dealings with the mafia and other unidentifiable individuals. The latter people in question seemed to always be linked to the disappearance of death of a reporter that got to close to the truth about Naira.

In 2025, the General in their timeline died of a brain tumor. That's when Naira made her move. She tried to have TTA and all their members assassinated, beginning with Sigma and yes, you guessed it, Val was there to stop them. Oddly enough, this 2kReturner didn't now this Val. So here's where things get more confusing.

This Val is a rogue TTA agent from their future. How far? Best estimate by the tech she used in our timeline? Give or take 20 or so years. She told Zyra that she was born in a world where Naira was the Supreme Ruler of both Earth and the Lunar Colonies. It started with my assassination and then the rest of my family. Events spiraled out of control from that point onward, leading to a vast police state that spread like a plague all across mankind's domain. Val's name to hide her true identity from her enemies was Valencia Valentine and preferred that everyone called her Val. Yet her real was Laina Avalon Daryl, the only child of Kayleen Evanston and Durk Daryl. Conner and Michelle Evanston were Kayleen's parents and Durk was Raynard and Jeanine Mellis' eldest son. Durk's youngest brother and only sibling was a famous, multi-talented athlete named Gordon. Strangely enough, Raynard didn't exist in our timeline. I hear he's quite the dancer just like Nin and Othelius are. Raynard and Jeanine established Club de Rayloria. In this timeline, Nina and Othelius started the same club. Yet we all knew the Club was a front for the Initiative.

So why does Val hate the Queen so much? UMOTE killed her parents in a terrorist attack on that Club in Sector B. There was one in every Sector but Sector B was exclusive to students. That being said, it was more luxurious than the other Raylorian Clubs in the other Sectors. Val was too young to know grief at that age when the new broke. She was 5. After the funeral, this happy little girl became a recluse. Her Aunt, Helen Ravenscraft, also a TTA agent, took care of her in her parents' absence. Val was a quiet individual but she had a thirst for knowledge. She wanted to know what really happened to her parents, not the lie her drunkard aunt told her. Helen sold Val the story that her parents were TTA agents on a long mission. Helen was to take care of Val while they were gone.

Val joined TTA to find them but when she found the truth, revenge and hatred for the Queen and anyone who supported her consumed this young lady. Val's new life's mission was to end Queen Adega, UMOTE, and anyone who stood in her way of accomplishing that. She was determined to get justice for her parents. The trail led her to UMOTE's leader, a man known publicly as Lord Ivon Emmanuel but to his enemies, Master Wongo.

Unfortunately, Val's mission wasn't approved by TTA and they forbade her to go after him. Shortly after her reprimand, Val went off the radar on a quest to personally deal with Master Wongo. She got close once and gave him that scar on his face but before she could finish the job, TTA showed up. Val escaped into the multiverse to avoid capture.

To me, Val didn't seem like a bad person. She so happened to save my friends, family and I on numerous occasions. TTA, however, doesn't see her as such.

Da heck?

Who said they could decide what events can happen and what couldn't?

If it hadn't been for Dr. Time, your sus lil' organization would've been stamped out by UMOTE! The nerve of you holier than thou punks! Now you hunt a woman who just wants her parents back? Unforgivable!

I see the nobility in Val's mission but speaking from experience, Val may never get them back. Her mission is all in vain. Even if she does, things won't be like what she remembered. And that's only if she'll remember anything about how things were at all.

As for this reality, at least the Initiative ended a tyrant's reign. If any rise up to take Queen Adega's place, regardless of what timeline they come from, we will deal with them like we dealt with her!

About the Author

Othello Gooden Jr. was born on January 13, 1985 in Cincinnati, Ohio. At an early age he learned the basics of reading, speaking, and writing while attending ministry school. Throughout his school years till now, he expressed those abilities in multiple online communities. Upon graduating from the School for Creative and Performing Arts in 2004, majoring in instrumental music, Othello enrolled in University of Cincinnati Raymond Walters College's Computer Support Technology program. While there, he learned the basics of MS Office, Object Programming, journalism, and animation. His passion for writing continued as Othello entertained his peers and teachers with his stories.

After graduating in 2009, Othello started creating videos on YouTube, first beginning with 2kReturner (gaming). The home of his stories' multiverse is on the Quantafilmationz channel. Here he vlogs about the background of each universe within the Travelers Frontier Multiverse. Also on this channel are animated shorts and web series. His flagship series is the Super Mecha Madness Show. It's a sci-fi stop motion animation that tells the story about a group of vigilantes living in Cyberspace known as the Super Mecha Team. The SMMS takes place within an alternate reality of the Rayloria's Memory book series universe. To date, Othello has reached an audience of over a million worldwide with his stories (across all mediums created).

Today, Othello continues to write stories (Music, Film, & New Media being an extension of that). As the artist known as JGTraveler, he's featured on several mixtapes, and has songs in major motion pictures & TV shows worldwide.

www.ingramcontent.com/pod-product-compliance
Ingram Content Group UK Ltd.
Pitfield, Milton Keynes, MK11 3LW, UK
UKHW061701190726
13853UKWH00008B/2349